THIS CANDLEWICK BOOK BELONGS TO:

_____

_____

_____

For Amy and Joe
D. M.

To Scott and Joan for all their work
V. G.

First paperback edition 2008

The Library of Congress has cataloged the hardcover edition as follows:

Martin, David, date.
All for pie, pie for all / David Martin ; illustrated by Valeri Gorbachev. —1st ed.
p.   cm.
Summary: Grandma Cat bakes an apple pie that is heartily enjoyed by her family
as well as the Mouse and Ant families that live nearby.
ISBN 978-0-7636-2393-7 (hardcover)
[1. Cats—Fiction. 2. Mice—Fiction. 3. Ants—Fiction 4. Pies—Fiction.]
I. Gorbachev, Valeri, ill. II. Title.
PZ7.M356817All 2006
[E]—dc22   2005046917

ISBN 978-0-7636-3891-7 (paperback)

2 4 6 8 10 9 7 5 3 1

Printed in Singapore

This book was typeset in Chesterfield D.
The illustrations were done in
ink and watercolor.

Candlewick Press
2067 Massachusetts Avenue
Cambridge, Massachusetts 02140

visit us at www.candlewick.com

All for Pie, Pie for All

David Martin   illustrated by Valeri Gorbachev

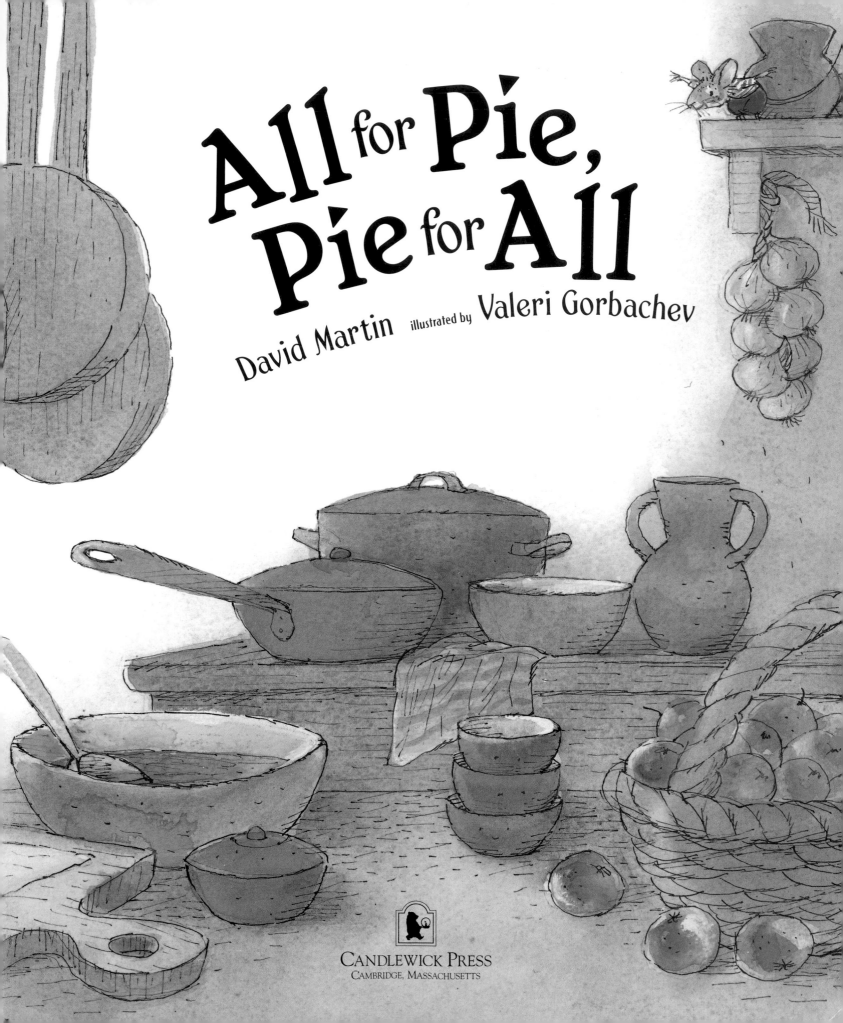

CANDLEWICK PRESS
CAMBRIDGE, MASSACHUSETTS

Grandma Cat made an apple pie.

Little Brother Cat ate a piece.
Big Sister Cat ate a piece.
Momma Cat ate a piece.
Poppa Cat ate a piece.
Grandma Cat ate a piece.

One piece of pie was left.

And then the cats took naps.

"I smell apple pie," said Grandma Mouse.

Little Brother Mouse ate a piece.
Big Sister Mouse ate a piece.
Momma Mouse ate a piece.
Poppa Mouse ate a piece.

Grandma Mouse ate a piece.
Six crumbs were left.

And then the mice took naps.

"I smell apple pie," said Grandma Ant.

Little Brother Ant walked away with a crumb.
Big Sister Ant walked away with a crumb.
Momma Ant walked away with a crumb.
Poppa Ant walked away with a crumb.
Grandma Ant walked away with a crumb.

One little crumb was left.

Then Baby Ant woke up from her nap.

"Pie!" said Baby Ant.

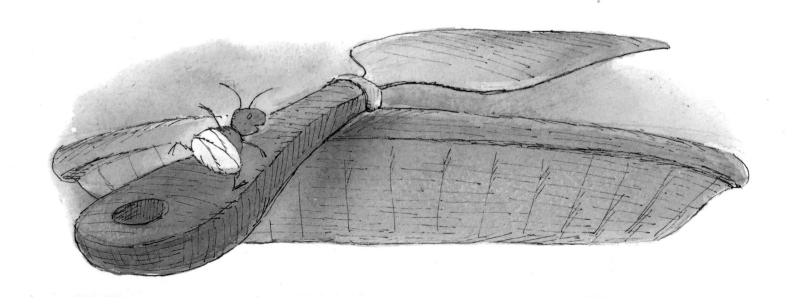

Baby Ant walked away with the last crumb.
Then the pie was all gone.

"I'm hungry. Should I bake another pie?" asked Grandma Cat.

"Yes. Yes. Yes. Yes," meowed the cats.

"Yes. Yes. Yes. Yes. Yes," squeaked the mice.

"Yes. Yes. Yes. Yes. Yes. Yes,"

yelled the ants as loud as they could.

So Grandma Cat baked another pie. This one was blueberry, and Brother Cat and Sister Cat and Brother Mouse and Sister Mouse and Brother Ant and Sister Ant and even little Baby Ant all helped make it.

And then everyone helped eat it,
until not even a crumb was left.

David Martin is the author of *We've All Got Bellybuttons!*, illustrated by Randy Cecil, and *Piggy and Dad Go Fishing*, illustrated by Frank Remkiewicz, among other books. Of the inspiration for *All for Pie, Pie for All*, he says, "I love to bake apple, peach, and blueberry pies. It always seems that after dessert there's one piece left. Then later the unseen nibblers get to work. Someone goes by and takes a little piece, and someone else takes another little piece, until finally it's all gone." David Martin lives in Vermont's Northeast Kingdom.

Valeri Gorbachev has written and illustrated many books for children, including *Goldilocks and the Three Bears*, which *School Library Journal* called "a perfect version for preschoolers." He also illustrated Sandra Horning's *The Giant Hug*. About *All for Pie, Pie for All*, he says, "The basic thing for an illustrator to do is to create a cozy, truthful world for the characters. That's what I've tried to do in this book." Valeri Gorbachev lives in Brooklyn, New York.